It's Party Time!

Lisa Bruce &
Susie Jenkin-Pearce

W
FRANKLIN WATTS
LONDON · SYDNEY

It was time for Joshua's party.

Becky met Bobby,
Sam and Neetu.
They had each brought a present.

Becky was excited.
She wanted to open one.
"It's Joshua's special day," said Mum.

"You'll have lots of presents when it's your birthday," she said.

"Let's play musical bumps,"
said Joshua's Mum.
Everybody danced.

Becky was good at bumping down.
Sam sat on a balloon. BANG!

"Time for tea now," called Joshua's Dad.

Becky ate until she couldn't fit another crisp in.

Everything went dark. In came Joshua's birthday cake with four shining candles on top.

With a big puff Joshua blew out all his candles.

Then Joshua's mum gave Becky
a HUGE parcel.
She wanted to open it.

"No Becky," said Mum, "you give it to Sam when the music starts."

The music stopped and Neetu
tore off the paper. Inside was
some more paper.

At last it was Becky's turn.
The parcel was very small.
"I've found the present," she yelled.

They played lots more games,
until it was time to go.
"Here's some cake to take home,"
said Joshua's Mum.

"Thank you for a lovely time," said Becky happily.

Can you guess what is inside these presents?

Sharing books with your child

Me and My World are a range of books for you to share with your child. Together you can look at the pictures and talk about the subject or story. Listening, looking and talking are the first vital stages in children's reading development, and lay the early foundation for good reading habits.

Talking about the pictures is the first step in involving children in the pages of a book, especially if the subject or story can be related to their own familiar world. When children can relate the matter in the book to their own experience, this can be used as a starting point for introducing new knowledge, whether it is counting, getting to know colours or finding out how other people live.

Gradually children will develop their listening and concentration skills as well as a sense of what a book is. Soon they will learn how a book works: that you turn the pages from right to left, and read the story from left to right on a double page. They start to realize that the black marks on the page have a meaning and that they relate to the pictures. Once children have grasped these basic essentials they will develop strategies for "decoding" the text such as matching words and pictures, and recognising the rhythm of the language in order to predict what comes next. Soon they will start to take on the role of an independent reader, handling and looking at books even if they can't yet read the words.

Most important of all, children should realize that books are a source of pleasure. This stems from your reading sessions which are times of mutual enjoyment and shared experience. It is then that children find the key to becoming real readers.

This edition 2003

Franklin Watts
96 Leonard Street,
London EC2A 4XD

Franklin Watts Australia
45-51 Huntley Street
Alexandria NSW 2015

ISBN 0 7496 4920 8

A CIP catalogue record for this book is available from the British Library
Dewey Classification 649

First published as *A Party* in the Early Worms series

Printed in Belgium

Consultant advice: Sue Robson and Alison Kelly,
Senior Lecturers in Education,
Faculty of Education, Early Childhood Centre,
Roehampton Institute, London.